Elijah
WRight

The SOUTH CAROLINA Night Before Christmas

E.J. Sullivan

Illustrated by
Ernie Eldredge

SWEETWATER
PRESS

SWEETWATER
PRESS

ISBN-13: 978-1-58173-396-9
ISBN-10: 1-58173-396-8

Printed in China

The SOUTH CAROLINA
Night Before
Christmas

'Twas a South Carolina night before Christmas,
    and from Greenville to Myrtle Beach,
Not a creature was stirring—even the shrimp were asleep.

Our stockings hung
on the porch, where
Santa could reach us
To fill 'em with NASCAR
stuff and all kinds
of peaches.

Baby Sister was snuggled all safe in her bed,
With visions of cheerleader practice in her head.
And me in my Tigers jammies, and Luke in his Gamecocks tee,
Were dreaming of touchdowns and playoff victory.

When out by the barbecue grill I heard a noise
        so loud,
It sounded kinda like the roar of an overtime crowd!

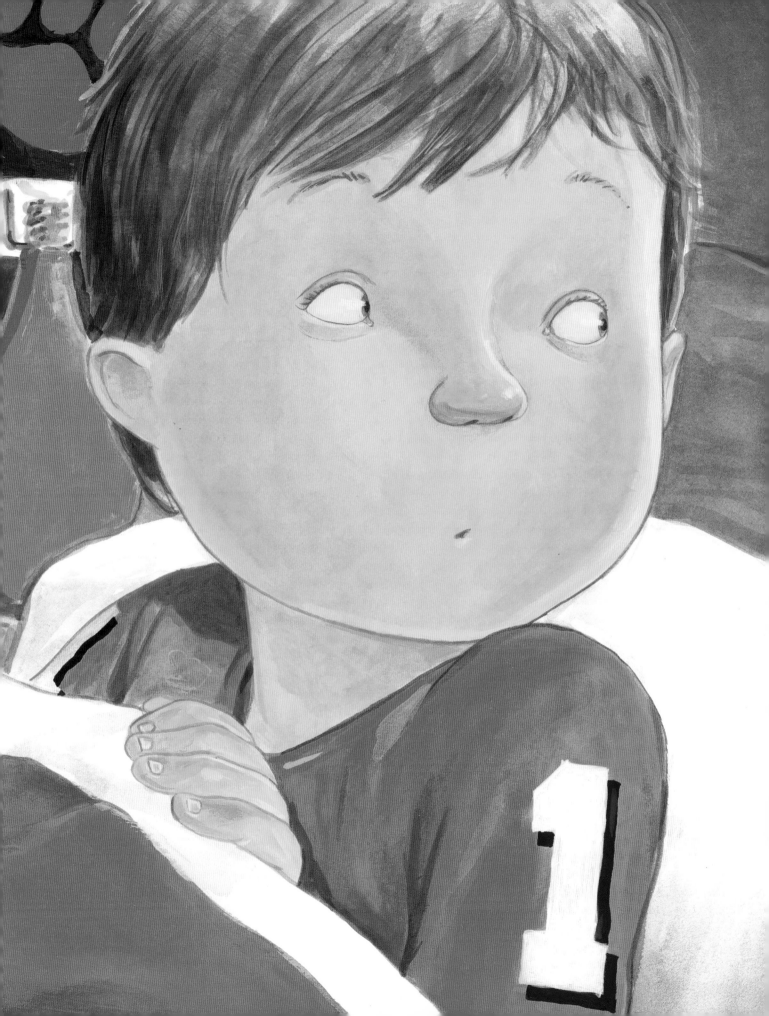

I sprang to the window and ran
down the stair,
Armed with Grampaw's autographed
Chubby Checker guitar!

The moon was as bright as the new dollar store
They put in down the road—it's open all hours!
And then what to my wondering eyes should I spy
But a great big ol' pickup truck flyin' on by...

With a little ol' driver so
lively 'n' quick,
He coulda made it 'round
Darlington ten times
in a lick!

Eight shag-dancin' reindeer was pullin'
   that contraption,
And he hollered so loud you could hear
   him in Charleston:

"On Dizzy, Darius, Jesse, and Strom!
Go Vanna and Leeza! Junior! Bubba get on!
From Hilton Head Island to Traveler's Rest,
Fly to Spartanburg and Columbia—you deer
   do your best!"

Υou know how when the weathermen come on TV
Screamin' that hurricanes are gonna blow us all away?
That's how crazy it felt watchin' that pickup zoom by me.
Got so worked up, I needed a glass of sweet tea!

As I finished my tea, I saw our palmetto tree shake
When the bottom of that peach truck started to scrape.
I looked up through the limbs and caught him red-handed—
On our Fort Sumter birdhouse Santa'd crash landed!

Bless his heart. He looked kinda like the Swamp Fox to me,
With his long hair and beard tangled up in that tree.
Mom's always saying I should help folks who are older,
So I helped him get down onto our John Deere mower.

Santa headed inside with our dog, Shoeless Joe,
And filled all our stockin's with peanuts and banjos.

Then he looked right at me, and before
going out the door
Slapped on top of the TV some
new bass fishin' lures.

Then he fired up his pickup and
	soon he was gone,
All the while telling those deer to git along.
But I heard him holler out as his rig
	sped away,
"Merry Christmas, South Carolina!
	I wish I could stay!"